CU01521491

EIGHTEEN

SHORT

STORIES

To Zach,

Thanks for the Support!

Shaun O'Reilly

x x x

COPYRIGHT © 2020 Shaun O'Reilly
All rights reserved.

No part of this publication may be reproduced, or transmitted, in any form or by any means, electronic, mechanical, photocopying, recording, or otherwise without the prior written permission of the author. Printed in The United States of America.

'We, the unwilling, led by the unknowing, are doing the impossible for the ungrateful. We have done so much, for so long, with so little, we are now qualified to do anything with nothing forever.'

Konstantin Josef Jireček

'He who has a why to live can bear almost any how'

Friedrich Nietzsche

'Stick it up your bollocks'

Roy Keane

Contents

THE WETHERSPOONS DOLE QUEUE.............................1

DARTS, WEED, FISH AND A NAIL GUN.........................9

THE RETIREMENT COMMUNITY...............................15

TWO OLD BOYS IN A PUB..19

NIGHT ON THE TOWN..23

MY MATE DAVE OF NO FIXED ABODE.......................31

IT'S A STRANGE OLD WORLD..................................37

I CHOKED ON A SAUSAGE......................................41

HOMELESS AND THE GIRL.....................................45

GOOD TIMES WITH GOOD MATES IN THE SMOKE53

DATE NIGHT AT THE ART GALLERY.........................57

A DAY IN THE LIFE OF BILL....................................59

CORONAVIRUS FILES #1..67

CORONAVIRUS FILES #2 STUPID OR GRATEFUL?....71

CORONAVIRUS FILES #3 CONFUSED.........................75

CORONAVIRUS FILES #4 SOCIAL MEDIA IS
BOLLOCKS...79

SHE ONLY FELT THIS WAY WHEN THE FULL MOON
WAS OUT..83

SCHOOL..87

The Wetherspoons Dole Queue

It was ten o'clock on a Monday morning and whilst most people were at work these two lazy pricks were sat in the Wood Green Wetherspoons nipping away on 'three-pound-fifty' pints of Heineken.

Scattered around the pub there were different types of patrons: The Old Boys drinking their cheap bitter, dressed up in suits and ties, married and widowed; then the construction workers drinking tea & coffee, eating the shit (but cheap) fry-ups that The Spoons churn out like a conveyer belt of cholesterol baiting heart attacks.

Few other dodgy types not drinking or eating - mostly meeting to discuss their nefarious actions for the upcoming week, like which variation of dodgy drugs to push. The pharmaceutical industry basically does the same as the North London heroin/coke pushing gangsters, but legally and on an infinitely larger scale. Figure that one out!

Our man Boris is thoroughly pissed off that he had an appointment at the Job Centre at nine AM this morning.

"These fucking spastic dickheads making me get up this early on a Monday is a fuckin' liberty. Had to be there for nine, which means getting up at eight, walk for two miles as the cunts don't give me enough to use the bus...

Then they tell me my benefits are being reduced as I could of taken the fucking fruit picking job in Bradford. Even though I told them I couldn't do it as I've got dodgy knees....

Also fucking told them for the thousandth time that I'm only looking for work in high-end politics. Tried to get me working on a bloody chicken farm last week, the cheeky cunts!"

Jeremy takes a sip of his pint and sighs inwardly. He just wants to finish his Sudoku in peace. He made the mistake a couple of weeks ago of indulging Boris in a conversation about the Cuban Missile Crisis and now this messy haired fool bothers him constantly.

It's a pain as he would happily change pubs, but The Spoons is cheap and on his doorstep.

Jeremy has a solid pension plan and has worked hard his whole life to get to the point where he can just chill the beans and spend his days in the pub in his own company, away from under his wife's feet. Now he finds himself getting hassled by this floppy haired tit every day. Whilst deep in thought about all this, he notices that Boris is still talking incessantly in his ear.

"The fucking thing is Jeremy, is this bloody Tory government. They don't give a shit about new working class cunts like me. Keep the rich rich and the poor under control. I told Sandra my work coach that at the Job Centre and she stared at me like I was a mad one."

Jeremy takes a mental note and realises that he hasn't actually said anything for ten minutes and Boris has just been ranting about socialism, and how Karl Marx had the right idea. Or something like that. He hasn't been listening. He also has a sneaking suspicion that Boris has been on the coke again.

Irritated by this bumbling mess in front of him, Jeremy walks off to the toilet. At least that'll afford him a few minutes peace. Pondering if he's happy or not, he always said he wanted to work hard his whole life so that when his retirement did come he could just spend his days nice and relaxed as an old man chilling out in pub with a good book and Sudoku. He didn't take into account that others in pub would be annoying the shit out of him.

Washing his hands thoroughly, as this new super bug has been in the news a lot and apparently attacks the older generation making them more vulnerable. Who knows what will come of that though...

Walking back into the pub, he's straight over to the bar as he doesn't want Boris to see him. He knows he'll try to blag a pint from him.

Too late as the tit is straight over, calling out...

"Jezza! Grab me a fucking pint while you're there...."

Seething inside, Jeremy nods in acquiescence to the barmaid. There's that reluctant acceptance without protest again that summed him up according to his wife. "When are you gonna stick up for yourself, Jeremy" ran through his tired old mind.

Strolling back with the two pints in his hands, placing them on the table, Boris grabs his with a vacant, mumbled "Cheers Bruv" roughly in Jeremy's direction, then continues back to his ranting about his reduction in his benefits.

"Every two fuckin' weeks I've got them bothering me. I had them pricks told right, I'm only accepting work in politics. Had to go to a job seekers meeting last week with all these other plebs. Some daft bint telling me about the interview process. Like I don't know!?"

Jeremy takes another swift sip on his pint and feels like he's got an annoying fly buzzing round his ear. Another bug bear is that this ignorant fool gets too close when he talks; he can feel bad breath and spit flying into his face...

"I said if you get me working on a chicken farm, I'll sue you lot for liable. And you can't stop me benefits as I would take the work if I could, but I can't. Fuck's sake - hang on; Donald's here......"

Jeremy exhales and visibly shakes at this arrival. He really can't stand this 'Yankee' ignoramus. Donald is an American guy who drinks in the pub and is known to the regulars. Fancies himself as a business man, but in reality he just sells stolen packets of ciggies and packaged meat, and anything he can nick out the back of Tesco.

Never stops talking about how great he is and all the deals he's gonna do - you know the type...

"Don't look up and the cunt might not see us", Boris whispers whilst turning around.

"HEY BOYS!" Donald screams and starts walking over...

Jeremy lets out a "Oh, for fuck sake. This twat again..." under his breath,. Boris mumbles something incoherently.

Strolling up in a scruffy long trampy-type jacket, Donald joins the three of them at the table and is straight on the selling.

"Line up you Limey scum... I've got 400 Benson & Hedges, a free-range chicken, four cans of Special Brew and a Mary Berry cookbook. A treat for the lady in your miserable lives. I'll do the lot for eighty bucks?"

"Nah, We're all fine mate. Shit off..." says Boris dismissively. Jeremy doesn't even acknowledge this new addition.

"Your loss boys" says Donald, a bit too loudly, then swans off bothering other people in the pub on this sunny Monday morning.

Boris takes a long drink from his pint.

"You do know that Yankee cunt is on the dole aswell! Plus I got a sneaky look at his records when I was in this morning. He's claiming disability as well as everything else! Gets more from the British benefit system than me! A man who has paid into the pot all his life! Well, most of it..."

Boris then proceeds to go on a coke and booze fuelled rant two inches from Jezza's ear about how if he was in government then there would never of been a recession and the economic effects of letting Americans into the UK.

Jeremy was beginning to feel the old rage bubble up beneath the surface, twenty minutes since that daft yank left and he's had this 'Mong' ranting in his ear and was at snapping point.

Boris's cocaine fuelled rant had found it's way into the flat earth conspiracy...

"The Evidence is there, Jezza! When you look out at sea you don't fucking see round. You see flat! Or on a plane, looking out the window, everything's fucking flat. So, logic would suggest that the earth is flat. It's a government lie to keep us under...."

At this point the old boy 'Jezza' had enough and in a blind rage he threw his half-full pint over Boris, head-butted him, threw a chair at a couple of randoms who looked up to see the kerfuffle, ripped up his Sudoku book and screamed "SHIT FUCKIN' FUCKER SHITHEAD TIT" and stormed out the pub.

Once the red mist had passed and his faculties and thoughts had returned to him, he reasoned that he should head over Hampstead way and find a nice, quiet, civilised pub away from this twat and his flat earth nonsense and that daft 'Yank' trying to sell him packets of bloody Spam every day.

A man of his age deserves peace in his retirement - not to be subjected to dribble from men like that. Taking out a Marlboro Red, he takes a long, deep inhale before wandering off into the dirty streets of Wood Green.

As he leaves he can hear Donald trying to sell a broken vacuum cleaner he found abandoned to a ninety-three year old, wheelchair-bound blind women with a one legged dog called 'Winston'.

Darts, Weed, Fish and A Nail Gun

Anxious to get out of the flat, all he could think of was how it was only supposed to be a mindless bit of fun. Wasn't supposed to be anywhere near as bad as it was. One of those moments in life where it all just ran away from him and all control of the situation seemed to be lost within an instant.

Sitting at the park bench opposite the cricket ground with shaky hands, he reached for his packet of smokes, lit one up and stared straight ahead thinking to himself how the feck he was gonna talk his way out of this one. Pulling his iPhone from his jacket pocket, straight onto Spotify, he found Slayer's Raining Blood album and pressed play.

As the extreme thrash metal blasted into his ears, he felt like he could finally think, unbeknownst to him why - but a smoke and a decent metal album always helped the old clarity kick in.

To be fair to him, who the fuck leaves a fire extinguisher and a nail gun in the front room anyway? Those two things are never gonna mix and it's gotta be her fault for leaving them in there.

'Her' was a Dutch girl who rented him the room in the flat share three weeks before, and just happened to be a weed smoking, obese, darts fanatic. With her practice dartboard up in the front room, she would spend hour after hour practicing her 501 game, smoking and stuffing junk food constantly into her face. Thirty-two left, double sixteen out was her favourite finish (in case you were wondering).

Along with the dartboard, the only other point of interest in the front room was the tropical fish tank. The Dutch girl seemed to be thoroughly enamored, with these rare tropical fish, the darts, weed, food and fish seeming to be the only thing she gave any kind of shit about.

She wasn't interested in keeping the flat clean. The dishes regularly piled up in the sink, the carpeting within the flat didn't even know what a vacuum cleaner was, the floors were littered with take away boxes of Domino's Pizza, and the place had a general stink to it. As a naturally sloth like creature himself, all these features in an abode and a person were appealing to him. Meaning that he had free reign to be a lazy sod with immunity.

Now 'Our Man' had settled into the gaffe well, made friends and even enjoyed the odd game of darts and an occasional joint with the obese Dutch girl. Things seemed to be going swimmingly - that is up until this particular night.

Leaving the pub at midnight after seven pints and a couple Jaeger Bombs, it's fair to say that he was fairly well buckled. Wobbling up the garden path to his new front door, scratching away at the lock, until the key found it's way into the hole.

Inside the house he saw the light on from underneath the door of his flat mate. Smelling that sweet skunk smell drift from the room and the sounds of Die Hard II blaring out, it's apparent she'd had a night in for one: skunk, action movies and (from the crunching sound) it was apparent she'd been grazing on a tube of beef flavoured Pringles.

Making a mental note of her nocturnal tidings, he wandered into the kitchen with the walls helping to hold him up, grabbed a can of Stella and settled in the front room, giving a drunken wave and tap on the glass to his favourite fish in the tropical tank.

Straight onto the sofa with phone in hand to see if he could find the girl he hazily remembered from the pub on Instagram. Worth a punt in giving her a 'Follow', he reasoned.

Now he never noticed this before, but the obese Dutch girl had used a nail gun to put the dartboard up. Obviously using a hammer to put it up was far too much like effort, and she had just discarded the nail gun lazily on the floor.

Realising that he'd never actually seen (let alone used) a nail gun before, he picked it up and gave it an inspection. Inspired by the sounds of Die Hard, the next thing he knows he's swiftly jumping around the front room, pointing the nail gun at imaginary, Nazi-type bad guys and imagining he's a prime Bruce Willis saving the world from the evil that men do.

After a solid two or three minutes of this, and practising his draw on several occasions, mumbling things like "Aster-La-vista Baby", he spotted the dartboard hanging seductively from the wall. His next imaginary scenario is that he's on stage at Ally Pally in the final of the Worlds Darts Championship.

Two thousand screaming, pissed up fans in fancy dress are roaring his name. Double sixteen is all he needs to take that trophy home and he'd be lauded as the best darts player ever to live!

Drawing the nail gun up and closing one eye, sight set completely in laser-focus on that red velvet looking double sixteen. Beads of sweat running down his head. He could hear the crowd holding their breath as one...

Completely in the moment he squeezes the trigger...

The nail gun goes off in his hand...

All in the space of a few seconds, quite a few things happened. A nail fired out of the gun, smashing into the dartboard from a distance of six feet, pinning it to the wall and leaving it hanging upside down with plaster and debris flying about the place. The retort of the gun going off shot it back, smashing him square in the nose, causing him to squeeze the trigger again, firing yet another nail into the fire extinguisher (which in turn explodes near the fish tank), which smashed, bringing a tsunami of water, glass and tropical fish on the floor, and the white-foamy-shite from the fire extinguisher. Obviously unaware the nail gun was plugged in, sparks started to fly out of the plug socket and an electrical-type fire threatened to light up. All-in-all, a pretty fucked situation I'm sure you'll agree.

Backing off towards the door with the nail gun still in hand, shaking at the situation that he'd been confronted with, he turned to see the obese Dutch girl in the frame of her door with Die Hard II still blaring from her bedroom. She was wearing a onesie with FEMINIST FOR LIFE printed on the front of it, and in one hand a half-smoked joint. In the other, a cold, crusty slice of Domino's...

"What the fuck's going on?" she wobbled out in a scared but confrontationally stoned voice, slightly anxious that he was clearly drunk and holding a nail gun.

"Ehmm, I'm really sorry. You can keep the deposit..."

Dropping the nail gun and bolting for the front door, he glanced into the front room for the last time to see his favourite fish flapping-to-fuck on the floor, surrounded by glass and foam.

Just as he slammed the front door, he heard a muffled scream from his ex-obese Dutch flat mate.

Was only having a laugh, for fuck's sake...

THE RETIREMENT COMMUNITY

All six hundred of the old folk were wandering around the retirement caravan park looking confused, while a dickhead with small man syndrome and a slight Nazi-ish vibe was standing at the front gates with a clipboard telling them they had to leave by four o'clock.

'But, we've got nowhere to go..." says an old wifey in a wobbly high-pitched voice, whilst holding her tiny dog (who also looked upset, both riddled to the dusty old bones with arthritis).

"I'm just following procedure, Mavis. Government and park officials are closing the park and we need everyone off by four. I don't make the rules - I just ensure they're followed. Next!"

"My wife is seventy-four and she's only just had her hip replaced a month ago. She can't walk, let alone move out..."

"I'm very sorry to hear that, Nigel. However, the rules and regulations state very clearly that during a global pandemic everyone, old or young, sick or well, need to vacate their holiday homes..." Heil.

"But we live here all year round and this has been my home for the past seventeen years. I'd have to live with my son. If I move in with him I'll get the virus and die a horrible, horrible, horrible death..."

"Once again, I'm sorry to hear that Edna, but rules are rules, and we can't bend them every time there's a pandemic or some of you might die. The protocol is there for a reason."

Another grand old gentlemen approaches with a monocle, a three-piece suit and pocket watch with a well-bred boxer dog called Cyril.

"I was in the Raj! The British Indian Empire and this is simply an outrage! The government is enforcing self-isolation and you mean to evict us from our homes, thus making us likely to catch this dreaded disease and, as Edna says, die horribly. The older generation are most at risk, you ignorant imbecile. I didn't survive two wars to deal with this nonsense!"

"As I said Major Tomkinson, rules are rules and they simply can not be bent."

This prick loves bit of power.

At this point an OAP called Keith, who used to be a bare knuckle fighter and pub landlord in Bethnal Green, walks up the clipboard Nazi, and in one fluid movement swings his walking stick at his head with a frightening velocity, essentially sparking our man clean out.

A wild round of applause calls out throughout the gathering crowd as the seniors were getting thoroughly pissed off with this jobsworth ignoramus.

A huddle of the elders formed and discussions were instant on what to do next.

Sweet old Edna suggested eating the clipboard Nazi in some sort of delicious stew or Jam, reasoning that with the oncoming Corona-apocalypse, food shortage might be of concern, and also her knees hurt getting to the shop these days.

Martial Law was suggested by Major Tomkinson, thereby giving him the power to shoot anyone under the age of sixty trying to get onto the park. A rule he always wanted to enforce.

A consensus was reached and it was decided that both these were bloody good ideas and that was that.

In the months that followed this incident...

The Major enjoyed his retirement drinking brandy with his dog Cyril. Firing warning shots at passing joggers with his WWII relic rifle gave him a new lease of life!

Edna thoroughly enjoyed the rest of her days making a variety of different stews and jams made from the clipboard Nazi, and anyone else the Major shot trying to get on the park.

Keith was lauded by the rest of retirement community for his heroic actions in saving the park from evil forces, and named Head Of State of their own little society.

A small caveat - Edna and Keith ended up moving into a caravan together, and Keith got first dibs on the stews and jams.

And they all lived happily ever after and weren't affected by Covid-19 at all.

The End.

TWO OLD BOYS IN A PUB

Just a quiet pub in North London, not all that much going on to be fair. The sort of establishment where a shandy is considered a cocktail, pork scratchings are the only thing on the menu and if you're under fifty and venture in...

The music stops, everyone lowers their pints, venomous stares with a hint of malice shoot out of conjunctivitis filled bloodshot eyes, the dog hides under the table with a howl and an old boy in a flat cap grumbles "Fuck sake... that's the peace and quiet gone... cunts."

That's how it feels anyway, and I'd prefer not to be accused of hyperbole. It's my story, dickhead...

However, on this day it's two o'clock in the afternoon and while most of the populace are still slaving away trying to keep their heads financially above water, the two old boys Trevor & Steve are sat at the bar pissing away their pension money on £3.50 pints of happy hour Fosters.

Joined only by Maggie (the sixty-two year-old barmaid from Dublin). She carries a limp, and a haggard face plastered with make-up.

Imagine if Dolly Parton hit the booze and recreational drugs far too hard for fifty-odd years, had been through three failed marriages, four kids, lived in a bedsit with homemade tattoos and had a day job in Gregg's. Then you'd get our Maggie. Salt of the earth she is!

The only noise in the pub is coming from Lola's gentle snoring - Lola being Trevor's old age, overweight Bulldog who after her walkies to the boozer and her daily can of John Smith's out of her favourite red bowl needed a nap.

All three of them are deep inside their own heads and conversation is kept to a minimum, save only for announcing that a trip to the toilet is imminent or calling up another pint from Maggie. Even then it's more of a variation of grunts and nods.

Trevor & Steve have known each other for so long that any small talk between them is considered futile and conversations should be interesting or not at all. It's borderline rude to fill the air with small talk at this point.

Three quarters of the way through his third pint and barely six words said between them, our old boy Trevor has a flash of inspiration whilst staring at his iPhone. His thought process for the past hour has made sense and has reached a beautiful crescendo!

Throwing his head back and pushing his chest out (without getting off the bar stool) both Steve and Maggie look up from their own thoughts as they both become aware that something's gonna be said - even Lola wakes with heavy eyes from the snooze and looks up at her keeper! The tension's almost too much before Trevor says...

".... There has to be aliens out there somewhere. Stands to reason because where's all this technology come from?"

Steve considers this for a moment or so, Lola goes back to sleep and Maggie just looks pissed off...

"Two more Fosters Maggie" Steve mumbles...

NIGHT ON THE TOWN

It was one of those sunny London evenings that only come around about ten times a year. With the sun beating down hard, even the haggard streets of Camden Town revealed a certain charm that seldom shows itself to the tourists, locals, punks, drug dealers and vagabonds. It left the populace with a smile. Usually in this neck of the woods you'd find people mildly psychotic, with a general air of 'get fucked-ness' but today, the night felt young and there was a general understanding that this particular evening should be taken advantage of.

He'd just finished work for the day and felt good. Jumping on his bike he cycled in the sunshine down through Kentish Town heading towards Camden and as was his custom, Jimmy called into the Black Heart for a cheeky pint of the 'Hells' and allowed himself a good forty five minutes with 'HP Lovecraft'. He didn't even know himself where this obsession with horror books had come from of late, but it always seemed more appropriate to read them in a decent metal pub with plenty of gargoyles, a premium lager and a healthy sound of doom in the background.

After an hour and two pints later he felt his leg vibrant. Pulling his phone from his pocket, he saw the familiar screen shot of Alice brighten up his phone

"Alright darlin'?"

Even after four years and a fair amount of hassle, headaches and heartaches, Jimmy still felt the tingle is his stomach when speaking to her.

"Hi babe – what you doing?"

"I've just finished work, about to unlock me bike. Was considering calling into the Black Heart for a pint", he said whilst signalling to barmaid to pull another one.

"Well, I was thinking as the suns out we should have a date night?"

"Banging. Black Heart for a drink, then I'll treat you to an Italian?

"Can we?"

"All over it. I'll be at the Black Heart in ten minutes."

Thirty minutes later she arrived with a smile and found Jimmy with his head in a book and half way through his beer. She knew he'd been there for at least an hour but chose to ignore the fact. They went through their respective days and enjoyed each other's company before heading out onto the streets of Camden.

The sun had calmed down now and they spent the next couple hours enjoying the food. Conversation, as ever, flowed between aggressive debates on the state of the premiership to whether Meat Loaf could ever compete with Bruce Springsteen. Jimmy then dragged the conversation to her recent promotion before it strayed in to the dangerous territory of politics.

After a beautiful meal and Alice giving him that look in regards to leaving a tip. They left and walked arm in arm back into the streets. The sun had gone now but left the humid air behind and night had fallen.

"Can we have a quick one in the Black Cap?"

"Really...?"

"Please!"

"Fuck me - alright then. It's a good job I love you."

Jimmy wasn't into to the Black Cap, as it was a notorious gay bar. Not that he had anything against the gay community but it wouldn't be his first choice. It had however been a nice evening and he wanted her to be happy.

After getting into the bar and ordering two pints of premium they got a seat. Alice smiled whilst Jimmy rolled his eyes as a cross-dressed cabaret act jumped up on the stage - all feather bows and brightly coloured corsets - then pranced around to Lady Gaga. As always one pint turns into three and Jimmy admittedly found himself relaxing and actually enjoying himself.

A conversation was struck up with a fifty-odd-year-old guy with glasses and a lazy leg from a mining accident. With the music being loud and the drink flowing, the slightly bizarre nature of the evening had taken an unexpected and interesting turn - until the incident...

Onstage, the cross-dressed cabaret act was reaching fever pitch - going hell for leather stripping to Night Fever. The whole bar was transfixed, clapping along as the performance was reaching its crescendo. All eyes were staring ahead, but out of the corner of his eye Jimmy saw the old miner reach over and drop something in Alice's drink.

He then proceeded to full-blown psychotic mode. Reaching over Alice, he tried his upmost to fucking batter the old boy. The music stopped, the act stopped dancing and every one in the bar looked over at this thirty year-old shaved head guy trying to pummel an old man with glasses and a wonky leg.

It didn't look good from the outside in - a pretty brutal case of gay bashing in there, third degree. Alice was utterly dumbfounded that her generally calm boyfriend would flip out in such a way and no idea of the preceding incident. Jimmy grabbed the offending glass whilst assaulting a windmill of punches and refused to let go of it, whilst being dragged out by the bouncers.

Out on the street, Jimmy was still losing it and, uncouthly trying to explain, threw a psychotic fog that the old boy had put something in his girls drink. The miner and Alice made their way outside, with her sending apologetic embarrassed looks at bouncers with a look of unbridled confusion on her face. Once the bouncers managed to make some sort of sense out of Jimmy's insane shouting, they gathered that he wasn't grabbing the glass to hit anyone with, but to prove his point that something had been put in there.

The Bouncer, Jimmy, and Alice stared intently at the glass with the old miner standing sheepishly in the background with a hand covering the left side of his face. With utter disbelief and amazement they saw an eyeball staring back at them from the bottom of a half full pint of Carlsberg Export. The bouncer started smiling to himself.

"Well, that's a new one on me!"

"What the actual fuck? Is that an eyeball?" Alice said, in genuine disbelief.

The absurdity of the situation revealed itself to Jimmy and, along with his dark sense of humour, actually started to laugh. All three then looked at the old miner with the wonky leg who was still holding the side of his face.

"I thought it would be funny", he said sheepishly, head down to the floor.

"Are you fucking mental?!

Why would putting a eyeball in someone you don't knows drink be funny?!"

Alice's own anger was beginning to rise. It would appear the miner lost an eye as well as getting a wonky leg in that accident all those years ago, and had a tendency to play practical jokes with his eyeball. Jimmy looked at the bouncer with a smile

"Sorry about all that ranting and raving mate."

"It's alright - I would of done the same."

He then grabbed Alice's arm gently and said, "probably best we call it a night love?"

With one last look at the old miner, she slowly set off towards the tube with confusion written all over her face. As they were walking off they heard the old miner shout.

"Any chance I could get my eye back?"

MY MATE DAVE OF NO FIXED ABODE

My mate 'Dave' of no fixed abode, in front of Sainsbury's or the tube station he would stand day in, day out. Nice chap.

Well, as nice as anyone can be with a solid heroin habit, drinking cans of Carlsberg Special Brew at 8:46am on a Monday morning whilst asking the debt ridden populace of Willesden Green for their hard-earned change. Everyone's got their place in society though I suppose.

A friend described him as "that homeless guy who looked like Jesus on crack".

He once told me that since everyone's using cards these days the spare change economy is going pure tits up. Hard to disagree with him to be fair.

"Morning Dave, You well?"

"Not facking really. The tube's fackin' closed today so I ain't gonna be earning shit all. Essential fackin' repairs apparently. These bloody TFL types need to realise they're costing people a fackin' living here..."

It always struck me as interesting how Dave treated begging like an actual job, In a previous conversation he told me that he was actually very good at it.

"I don't make people feel fackin' awkward you see. If they say 'no', I say 'have a nice day' and then call them a cunt out of earshot, nice to be nice you see...."

He doesn't have a dog either as he feels it wouldn't fair on the little fella. Seen too many of his 'no fixed abode' mates unable to look after them, and doesn't like the idea of not being able to give them the best life - although the companionship would be welcome he admitted.

Couple of memorable events with my mate 'Homeless Dave'...

First involving the front wheel of my bike and the second involved an act of compassion with a drunk girl after a night out. We'll go with the bike first...

"Alright Dave, I'm just heading into McGowan's to watch Newcastle vs Arsenal. Got my new bike though. If I throw you a fiver, any chance you keep an eye on it? I've had two bikes nicked already this year."

That wasn't true, and I had a full-blown bomb proof lock on the bike to stop it getting nicked. However it's nice to give him a job. Thought being, it's nice to feel like you've got some self-worth.

"I'll take the fackin' work, Clapton. A lot on though today...."

(He always called me Clapton, as more often than not I had a guitar on my back).

He said this with the air of a man who was very busy but willing to do me a favour, this one time.

"I'll fackin' tell ya though that any thief worth his fackin' salt could steal that bike in ten seconds flat. I'll show you. It's all about the quick release front wheel."

Dave then proceeded to basically rip the front wheel off my bike...

"Told ya. Piece of fackin piss!"

"Thanks for showing me you can nick my front wheel, Dave, Any chance you could put the fucking thing back on my bike though? Kick off's in five...."

We then spent the next 20 minutes trying to get the wheel back on the bike as it turns out he somehow bent the bloody wheel taking it off. Cost me £80 getting a new wheel as I couldn't ride the thing straight after. Best fiver I ever spent that.

Dave's act of compassion with the drunk girl next....

The phone rings at 2am with the girl's name flashing up. Answer to check she's alright and I hear the kind of voice that would belong to a packet of Marlboro Red, some gravel covered in petrol and a brick that's been pissed on by a cat (if such a thing could have a voice).

"Alright Clapton. I'm taking ya fackin' bird home ya MUG!"

"WHAT? Who the fucks this?!"

"Dave...."

"Who the fuck's Dave?!"

"Homeless Dave, ya fackin idiot. You ain't got the brains you were born with. She's a bit worse for wear innit. Making sure she's safe ain't I. Dodgy round this fackin' manor at night..."

"Oh right... thanks for that mate, appreciate it!"

Ten minutes later I'm opening the door to a drunk girl and a homeless man.

True to his word she's safe and sound. Didn't have any cash on me so I gave him a box of chocolate eclairs and two cans of shit cider that had been in the fridge for months by way of payment.

Off he went well happy, job well done on his behalf.

Nice bloke Dave. Wonder what he's up to....

IT'S A STRANGE OLD WORLD

Stepping off the tube at Victoria, sweating buckets and regretting that sixth pint of Camden Pale Ale the night before. Literally thousands of people bombing about, faces stuck on their screen. You sometimes wonder if a ten tonne truck came steaming through the middle of them all, with little Korean huskies singing the hits of the 90s using only pan pipes, would anyone notice or even give a shit, let alone drag their faces out the soul sucking, swirling vortex that is the smart phone!?

Craving a cigarette but harshly reminding himself he quit, he wanders out onto the street and into the harsh realities of a Central London Wednesday morning. The usual madness occurring - homeless people lying on the street with a disused Starbucks cup, literally begging for pennies from city boy dickheads, strolling past giving off a vendor of money whilst - in reality - they're all ball deep in debt - overdraft, loans - just trying to keep up with the elite.

It's a strange old world and we must not forget the royal family only live up the road in their own gaffe. Protected by men in funny hats with bayonets whilst tourists, crack heads and used car sales men all stand outside Liz's big shiny walls. It's a strange old world...

Clutching the guitar strongly with his coat up against the wind, he heads towards the bus station. 9:46am and the coach to Lille leaves at 10. Head down, no more time to fuck about. Strolling down the busy road, people swarm like worker ants all around him.

Every single one of them with a story to tell. The blonde girl walking towards him in the Armani suit and Jimmy Choo shoes. She's on the brink of a divorce and literally can't stand the touch of her husband - only staying with him as she knows he's worth half a mill and needs to get her legal shit together before running off to Portugal with Carlos (the slightly overweight dullard who works in some shit pub in Kilburn).

Or the early twenties Chinese kid four steps behind her. He just moved to London after landing a job here with Apple. He's absolutely full of wonder and can't believe his luck that he's here - every site blowing his mind and he almost cried when he saw the Millennium wheel. Such a marvel of modern engineering. He can send money back to his family, and that alone fills him with a sense of incredible pride. Up there with the happiest man in the world, him.

Or the Christian man standing at the entrance to the coach station. "Jesus is lord. We must repent our sins, or Hell awaits you!" This bloke has got a secret fetish where he desperately wants other Christian men to drip candle wax on his balls and whip him with a leather strap whilst preaching the scientology rules, in some sort of bizarre rebellion against his maker.

All of this could be true, or on the other hand, none of it could be. Who knows? He just made it up to make the walk more interesting... and it worked. Truth is stranger than fiction sometimes so I'll stick with my own. Thanking you kindly...

9:52am. Gate 11. The line is moving and the bags are getting lumped into the bowels of the FlixBus. Pondering if he's got time to grab a cuppa of

Yorkshire Gold to help ease into the six-hour journey ahead, he's feels the vibration in his pocket and see's the familiar face of 'Frenchy' light up his phone.

"Safe travels, See you soon xx "

Smiling now at the thought of what's lying ahead, he decides against the brew as it could up the chances of being sat next to some smelly twat all day. An individual seat is paramount, overriding the need for that Yorkshire goodness.

9:56am. Showing the driver the e-ticket from his phone he finds two empty seats, wedges the guitar case into the empty one next to him (essentially stopping any smelly twat from get any ideas of sitting there), pulls out his tales of everyday madness and places it to the side before texting 'Frenchy' a picture of himself looking like a fat headed twat with a smile on his face.

10:00am. Rolling out of this town for a few days adventure. The hangover's a distant memory already. Happy days. Fucking wishes he had a cuppa Yorkshire goodness now...

I CHOKED ON A SAUSAGE

Nobody ever wants to finish a 10-hour workday and then nearly choke to death on the first bite of a 'Taste The Difference' sausage that they nicked from Sainsbury's, but sometimes it happens so just deal with it.

Karma really is a bitch to be fair. I suppose the moral of the story is "don't steal", but with the self-service checkouts these days and the bored-as-shite employers that suffer through their 8-hour shifts at these supermarkets, it's easily done.

After the longest day and the six mile cycle in the pissing rain all he wanted to do was eat and get into bed with a record playing and a decent book – but, as The Rolling Stones have taught us, you can't always get what you want.

Instead it was two days in a North London Hospital, vomiting constantly whilst being poked, prodded, sharp needles stealing blood, a drip and sleeping next to a Tottenham football hooligan with a dodgy heart (who, by his own admission, had voices in his head telling him shave the nurses long flowing black hair and wear her bog-standard NHS dress).

Not the most tranquil of environments when you can't breathe because you choked on a stolen sausage.

After the first bite it was apparent something wasn't right. The instant feeling of the throat closing in on itself and the panic of a burning sensation and that crippling inability to breathe; a swift kick in the bollocks would of been preferable to that feeling, although neither is ideal to be fair.

An hour later he's in the back of an ambulance spewing up and shaking like a shitting dog as the paramedics are trying to convince him its some kind of instant food poisoning whilst the housemate's telling the Scottish girl that her boy is in an ambulance because he's choking on sausage he nicked. He's a keeper this one...

A day later (still in the hospital) he's lying on his side while an amazing Indian doctor is forcing a camera down his throat and into the stomach just to confirm the fact the he's feckin' idiot incapable of chewing his food.

Even chimps have mastered this chewing thing and as a thirty four year old kleptomaniac you're still struggling. Dickhead.

This was what the doctor was thinking – however, it was verbalised as:

"The oesophagus is 75% inflamed and unable to hold any food or liquid for another day or so until the inflammation is reduced. You'll be put on another drip for 24-hours to keep you hydrated...." You're also an idiot...."

Back in the ward the lovely Scottish girl arrives with supplies and piles of moral support. The parents also arrive unannounced. It's the first time they've met.

Niceties are exchanged whilst he's in a chair white as a sheet, constantly throwing up into a bucket, clothed in a hospital gown with his arse hanging out and on a drip. As previously mentioned, he's a keeper this one...

A day later he's being discharged but under strict doctors orders. No alcohol. Tablets twice a day for two months and learn to chew your bloody food, you egregious bloody fool.

People smarter than you have have died from this. Have a nice day. Now shit off...

HOMELESS AND THE GIRL

She stared at him with a vicious, open-eyed look of unadulterated anger. Then, as always, she chose to bite the bile down and fight the rage that was always bubbling underneath the surface. 'Choose your moment', she thought. It was the fourth time this week that the slimy prick had groped her on the tube. Travelling from her affluent suburb of Chiswick all along the Piccadilly Line up towards the piss bin that she worked at... Turnpike Lane.

Her husband was always saying that she didn't need to work and that he could pay for them both - however she just couldn't stand the glee in his voice, and the idea of her being a kept woman made her want to cut off one of his ears and make him eat it. She saw that in a film once and it always stayed with her. Johnny wasn't a bad guy, but at the end of the day he was a city boy prick who worked as a marketing executive (which we all know basically makes him somewhat of a cunt). She felt no remorse in these thoughts; just a slight disappointment in herself that she agreed to marry him and knew that it was only a matter of time before it all went tits up... even if that Johnny 'Wanker' couldn't see it just yet.

Hence this bullshit job in this bullshit bank in this bullshit area. Life wasn't quite what she planned out and at 33 years old she felt that she lost her way. Like a train going slightly off-course for 10 years ends up fecking miles away from where it's actually going but no one notices, until the conductor's kicking you off and calling you a twat for missing your stop.

Lost in her thoughts and the deafening screeching of the tube screaming she sees the slimy prick is wearing an overly tight black top with his hair gelled and combed back, basically trying to put himself across as a gangster. Glancing up she sees that they've just past King's Cross and gratefully thinks that she's only 4 more stops before he gets off at Finsbury Park. Only four more stops to avoid his disgusting glare, she sees him looking her legs up and down and feels like he's mentally undressing her bog standard Lloyds outfit, starting with her dress.

She begins to retch at the thought of this piece of shit doing this to her. The retching begins to pass, however, and is replaced with a blind rage as they meet eyes. He smirks. She looks away, then looks up and catches his eye again. Gently she fingers the orange Lucozade bottle that she put in her handbag last night after the city boy wanker husband had gone to bed at 9.30pm as he needed a good night sleep because his boss from San Fran was in town.

The beautiful rich Japanese-looking girl that he never stopped talking about these days. She knew he hadn't fucked her yet but would literally shit on demand if she said, so it was probably on the cards. It wasn't the inevitable affair that he was going to have - more the anger at herself for falling into the bullshit rat race. Yet, as her dear old dad had told her on her last visit to Belmarsh Prison, "It's never too late to surprise yourself or put some cunt in his place darlin'." She knew her old man was a grade A lunatic but loved him for it. She also knew she was the only person in the world that he remotely cared about and her next actions would make him - and only him mind - very proud. Like any daddy's girl she couldn't help smile at the thought.

She stares up again sees the blue and red sign with "Finsbury Park" on it zoom by several times in a blur. She feels the slimy prick's gaze burning into the top of her head but won't give him the satisfaction of catching his eye. The spastic actually thinks that she might be somehow flattered or turned on by his moronic gaze or his early morning pawing at her arse. 4 times this week. 4-fucking-times this week and twice the week before this slimy prick had grabbed her arse.

The rage was rising again at her own thoughts – however, it quickly turned to a calculated psychotic calm that she knew for a fact she got from her dear old Dad. It was moments like this that she felt closest to him. Even though he was banged up and had no idea of her ongoing situation, she could almost feel him in her ear saying "Go on Sweetheart...." in his raspy cockney villain tone that she always felt so relived at hearing.

Managing to avoid his eyes, she calmly and gracefully grabs her bag and follows the slimy prick out of the tube. Blending into the crowd but keeping a trained eye on the prick, she follows him off the escalator and through the gates out into Finsbury Park bus station. Feeling her heartbeat rise but biting it down again and keeping the psychotic calm that she had grown to feel accustomed in.

She stealthily walked a good twenty steps behind him and followed him into the park left out of the station. She sees him walk past the homeless guy she always had a respect for. The man who literally had nothing but always kept his little space under the bridge tidy, well thought out, with his homeless bed folded neatly.

Not even surprised when the slimy prick glanced disdainfully at the homeless man and smirked at him in a way saying of you're beneath me. This only cemented that what she was about to do was not only right for society but for the good of the species. Or, if she was honest, she just wanted to watch this pricks face burn.

She toyed with the philosophy that people like her and her dad were built this way to kill off the ones that needed to be killed off for the greater good. Pondering the ethics of this philosophyas she conscientiously slipped her homeless man a tenner with a brief glance, whilst also trying to ignore his look of sadness that he knew she didn't have time for a chat this morning.

The homeless man looked forward to that every morning - in fact he got up and tidied his patch under the bridge especially knowing the pretty girl would walk past at 8.30am each day. He wanted nothing - the tenner a day, helpful as it was, would've been excused just for a chat. Highlight of his day it was. She made him feel human and he could also see the dark side in her, which he also had. His clearly getting the better of him, as he'd fucked up every opportunity given to him and was now living under a bridge, whereas she had all the trappings of a perfect life by the 'normal standards'.

She followed the slimy prick into the park whilst gently fingering the Lucozade bottle, relishing in that peaceful calm before the storm that she had often heard the old man talk about as a young girl. Even through his whiskey mumblings, she understood and felt like she'd experienced that same feeling without ever feeling it.

10 steps ahead, the slimy prick feels a sense of another human behind him and stops and turns. To her eye she sees a moronic reptilian idiotic smile staring back at her. He then takes 8 of those steps back towards her - her heartbeat rising, but once again biting it down, she snatched the bottle from her pocket, rips off the screw cap and throws the acid straight in his face.

Watching with a kind of morbid fascination as the slimy prick screams and rolls around the path grabbing his face, reveling in the steam and burning flesh as it fills her lungs, she calmly looks around and can't see a single soul. Unusual as it was, but very much aware that this is a golden opportunity to get away without witnesses, she calmly continues her walk towards the bullshit job in the bullshit bank.

Walking the rest of the way through the park and hearing the sirens screaming through the London air, she felt rejuvenated for the first time in a while. With a spring in her step and a certain weight off her mind, the rest of the day seemed like it should be taken advantage of. Burn the living shit out of some bridges - starting off with that tit of a husband. Maybe not burn his face but finish it with a 'It's not you, It's me' speech.

'Today is the first day of the rest of your life' fell into her head from somewhere, Always sounded like bollocks until today.....

GOOD TIMES WITH GOOD MATES IN THE SMOKE

Good times with good mates in the smoke. Some philosopher once said that 'there's always space in the your life to squeeze a couple pints in with your mates' – or, maybe I just made that up... quite possibly.

Record shops. A quick bomb around Highgate Cemetery. Bert Jansch has a resting place there. Legend. No one else seemed to give a bollocks - more interested in Karl Marx. Loved and hated to this day it seems is 'Old Karl'.

Swift pint in the 'The Flask' and a debate about whether Mr. Marx was some Robin Hood-type or just some ideologue aiming for some kind of utopian society that could never be reached

"Would never work lads. Utopia has an inherently contradictory nature."

The Big Man takes a thoughtful sip from his pint of London Pride.

"We're not homogenous as a society, and have desires which conflict and therefore cannot simultaneously be satisfied."

What is this bell end talking about?

"What the bollocks are you on about? Why aren't we talking about how Joshua's gonna do Klitschko..?"

"Fair point...."

"I reckon Joshua's got to nullify his jab and grab style. He ain't out box him like Fury did eighteen months ago. Slip the straight right and come up that demonic uppercut that did Dillian Whyte."

Evil Pete looks at both his mates and shakes his head.

"You're both such geeky twats in your own weird ways... it's never boring!"

The usual routine is occurring – the five or so minutes on family and work life, niceties concluded, straight onto the state of the Premiership and failing love lives.

Over the fourteen or so years of this friendship there's always one of the three who has fired into singledom and in the mist of some Jeremy Kyle-esque vibe.

Drink up and leave.

Walking down Highgate Hill, the air feels warm and the millionaires' houses jump out from the street. English countryside vibe up and down all day long here.

Ten minute walk and you're in Kentish Town surrounded by the crazies, the piss heads and belligerent thieves. Still never quite figured out how in old London town one minute you're in an affluent 'Harry Potter posh-twatty' suburb and the next you've found yourself in a 'moped-is-king stab city'.

It's a funny old world.

Settled into the new boozer in the shit part of town with a big screen to watch the big men punch lumps out of each other with your best mates. Happy days...

Post-war record crowd of 90,000 in attendance at sunny Wembley and about 200 at this dodgy bar in North London.

First four rounds close and neither fighter giving much away...

In the fifth, Joshua floored Klitschko...

In the sixth, Klitschko floored Joshua...

Eleventh, Joshua knocks him out on his feet!

Park Life blasts through the bar as pints, tables, small dogs, small humans fly through the air.

Spurs, Gooners, Tories and Corbynites are even being nice to each other. Never happens.

Jumping all over Evil Pete as he's wrestled to the ground while The Big Man is pulling us both up.

This ain't a normal Saturday night and it's known.

Good times with good mates in the smoke.

DATE NIGHT AT THE ART GALLERY

What's that dopey looking thing? Mona Lisa. Mona bloody Lisa! What sort of a name is that? Mona - maybe she moans that he never replaced the toilet roll after it was finished, or that he never took the bins out!

Can never get any peace. Even at the art gallery, Always getting grief. Feck this - I'm off.

"Sharon. Bollocks to this - this Mona Lisa thing is giving me the hump..."

She starts to moan aswell...

"It's date night? Why have you got to ruin everything, blah, blah, blah."

It's enough to give me the hump. I try to rationally explain that it's clearly not my fault and that if that 'Mona Lisa' wasn't whinging to me about the bins then we could have had a perfectly nice day. Same rules apply. She feckin' stares at me like a dog that's been shown a card trick.

"Are you on acid again?"

Cheek on her! I haven't done that in weeks and I only bastard well did it to find myself for her. Selfish her all over... I mean it's not my twattin' fault that the bloody unicorns wouldn't stop following me about and banging on about how Stuart Pearce was a seminal part of the Euro '96 line up. I feckin' told that 'Unicorn Gary' and his Orangutan mate that he didn't need to tell me that. Old psycho Stuart was a childhood hero of mine. Classic left-back!

Either way, I dragged her out and I'm heading to the Toucan. A pint of the black gold barkeep. Better chuck a nip in aswell. Whiskey helps me brain from overloading. Also gotta keep that 'Unicorn Gary' prick at bay. Don't fancy discussing the merits of the 96/97 season today - and especially not in this boozer with a Unicorn.

She's still moaning... Mona Lisa...

A Day in The Life of Bill

Bill was a nice guy who worked in his local Tesco on the fruit and veg section. He lived at home with his sixty-eight year old mother, who hadn't left the house for seventeen years.

The main reason she hadn't left the house for all those years was that she was regularly chained to the radiator.

What..? Sorry - jumped the gun there. Read on and all will be revealed...

Completely inoffensive, the type of chap who wouldn't say boo to a goose, and if he did would probably apologise and leave a fiver in an envelope. The goose would probably spend it on crack and cat nip, so I don't know why he would bother.

No one ever had a bad word to say about Bill – mainly because he hardly spoke and was so bloody boring that it would be similar to head-butting a fax machine in front of a love interest to impress the poor girl.

There's simply no point. The love interest would think you're a bit of a lunatic for head-butting an inanimate object, and the fax machine wouldn't even acknowledge or report the assault, as confrontation isn't in it's nature and you'd just end up looking like a right dick with a sore head.

The point I'm trying to make is that Bill was an exceedingly boring man that didn't stand out. Also, no one uses fax machines anymore.

He had no friends and had never been out of the small town that he was spawned in. Never had a girlfriend, or boyfriend. Never had any kind of relationship, therefore no one can accurately say which way his nocturnal behaviour leaned.

Could be gay or straight. Never showed any interest in the local floozy, or the only gay in the village, so your guess is as good as mine.

That's pretty much about it from your average guy on the street's perspective in regards to Bill. Locals knew who he was, but no one gave a pair of bollocks (because, why would they).

The day started off like any other. The town went about its morning business. The paperboy did his rounds, the beer delivery turned up at The King's Head and the commuters were heading out the door for another day of dreary nothingness.

After a twelve-hour night shift, our man Bill was wandering home. The same route he always took: left out of Tesco, right at the crossroads and straight onto Dollis Hill Road for thirty minutes until arriving at his ram-shackle cul-de-sac on the outskirts.

Putting his key in the lock of the front door, nothing felt different and his brain was just contemplating which shitty microwavable ready meal he was going to feast on with Mother.

Another side note is Bill only ever ate microwavable food - reason being, he had to feed Mother too, and didn't know how to cook.

Inside the front door he walked, unzipping his coat and hanging it in the usual place in the hallway. He strolled into the living room with his head characteristically bowed.

Making his way to the kitchen, he heard a mild, frightened shriek – a bit like a cry for help but from the mouth of a person who is almost too scared to draw attention. Bill stopped in his tracks - a cold, dead, sweating fear began to rise, starting in his bowels and slowly reaching up towards his chest, finding it's way to his throat.

"Is that you? We've been waiting on a feeding. Feckin' get in here boy. Got this hound dog chained up here with me!"

Now then, dear reader - only one of the things I'm going to describe to you next was surprising and upsetting to Bill. However, I'd confidently say that both of them will be to you, so please exercise caution and put your seat belt on.

Stepping slowly into the kitchen without looking up, Bill was acutely aware of two presences, where there would usually be just one.

Looking up, he saw dearest mother (clothed in her usual attire - we'll get to that), and what can aptly be described as a nice, god-fearing man, shaking and clutching literature on the Jehovah's Witnesses' faith in one hand, whilst the other was hand-cuffed to Mother (who was, as usual, chained to the heavy-set kitchen radiator).

Now, you'll be requiring some backstory to be able to make sense of the scene just described. You see, Bill's Mother was slightly – actually, utterly – mental.

After the death of her favourite singer Elvis Presley, she had spent every day dressing up as her hero. The wig, the glasses, the big frilly white jump suit. The whole shebang. Insisting to anyone that would listen that he wasn't dead, and that the whole thing was a conspiracy - a cover up as such - after being ostracised by all her family and friends, she became a full-blown recluse, refusing to leave the house and handcuffed herself to the radiator in protest between the hours of 9am-5pm every week day (she kept the key to handcuffs in the wig).

Now, when the nice man knocked on Bill's front door to preach the will of His Lord and Saviour on the morning of 6th June, Mother uncuffed herself, thoroughly irritated that her protest had been interrupted.

The harmless chap was met, and invited in, by an agitated old lady in full Elvis clobber, and offered a cup of tea and a piece of cake. Accepting that this was weird but remembering to "judge ye not", he kindly accepted. Plus he had been told to "shit off" six times already.

Coaxing him into the kitchen, she strolled over to the drawer next to the sink to grab the spare set of handcuffs, and in one swift movement wrapped the handcuff around his wrist, attaching the other end to her wrist - thus joining them in union.

With him frozen in shock and her still thoroughly irritated at the interruption, she proceeded to assume her usual position and handcuff her other hand to the radiator. Then she began to scream about how he was a "very naughty boy", and how he would be joining the protest that Elvis clearly wasn't deceased.

Bill knew better than to upset Mother when she was in this state, as - unsurprisingly enough - it wasn't the first time she'd taken a hostage and forced them to sit in her protest against The King's death.

Lets see now... there was the milkman a couple months back, the postman last year, that young charity girl; oh - and Steve (the Amazon Prime delivery guy, who strangely enough had joined her intentionally a few separate times).

Politely nodding with an apologetic smile to the god-fearing man, Bill proceeded to get the lucky dip of microwavable ready meals from the stock pile in the cupboard and popped the kettle on.

After breakfasting, and a formal announcement from Mother saying she would "let the nice man go at five o'clock", Bill gave an apologetic shrug to the

Jehovah's Witness and off to bed he went to get his beauty sleep for the evening's Tesco shift.

A few hours kip later (and a naughty dream about kidnapping and chaining Sandra Bullock to the Kitchen radiator), Bill awoke and made his way downstairs to find Mother in her favourite chair watching re-runs of Bargain Hunt with a brew. She also happened to be perusing some literature on the Jehovah's Witnesses.

"Hello boy. Nice sleep? I knocked off an hour early today and let that dickhead go. He kept crying and praying. Bloody well had enough of his whimpering. There's a fish pie in the microwave for you."

Bill joined his Mother in front of TV before heading out on his daily pilgrimage to his second fruit & veg-stacking shift of the week.

Not a lot else happened that week.

CORONAVIRUS FILES #1

This bloody Coronavirus ain't half a pain in the feckin' arse.

Within the space of three days all the work went down the shitter. All gigs cancelled as Boris closed all the bloody pubs, no teaching work as all the schools are closed.

That was me snookered: "Sorry lads, can't pay the rent so I'm off to live in the Old Dear's caravan with a Scottish girl who's got an actual job. Tell the landlord I said sorry but the money's gone old chap!"

Can imagine all the school kids loving it. Treating it like a snow day and a chance to kill off the older generation. If they play their cards right it'll be Xbox,

PornHub, Candy Crush and Chocolate to fill the days. Bollocks to your Geography lessons, ya old mugs.

I read of the butterfly effect once. The idea being that a butterfly flaps it's wings in the mountains of South Africa and a year later everyone in Clapham is speaking Japanese with tin foil sombreros on their heads worshipping midgets as Greek Gods. Think that's mental then let's try this one...

A nice man eats a bat in China and a few months later everything is utterly fucked worldwide. No planes in the sky, supermarkets empty, no one's allowed within two metres of each other, gotta stay inside ya Mum's caravan for two/three months. It's a mental old time sure enough...

Kinda all started in the taxi back from Dublin to the airport. The taxi's radio rattles out in that wirey sound.

"All pubs and bars are now officially closed and public meetings are banned."

Looking at the Scottish girl I'm thinking, but it turns out I'm verbalising.

"Would you ever of thought that there would come a time in history when every single pub in Ireland would be closed for the foreseeable future?"

That's when it hit home I suppose. Nothing ever really does hit home until it affects you directly I've heard it said, and closing every pub in Ireland definitely was a sledgehammer in the tits. Who'd have a thought it?

Back in London and in another taxi it's abundantly clear that England's yet to catch up on how serious this is. Asking the driver the score, he's croaking "not a lot's any different to be honest. Load of old nonsense if you ask me!"

The next day, football's gone for the season - Liverpool & Klopp are bloody fuming. Hard luck boys, maybe next year. Can hear the laughs coming out of Manchester. Literally the only thing fucking up the title for Liverpool is a global pandemic! Here ya go lads, one global pandemic as ordered...

Every afternoon at five the nation is standing still as old Boris tells us in so many words that we're all fucked, standing proud and channeling his best inner Churchill (filtered through his Eton tongue).

"Pretty much you're all gonna lose ya jobs and the lucky ones are gonna get furloughed. Oh, and stop going out. You're all bloody grounded until this shite blows over. Play nicely at Marks & Sparks... I'm off for shit!"

Oddly enough, Boris caught the bloody virus and had to self-isolate himself. No exceptions apparently. The scruffy-haired PM is running the country from a small flat above Number 11 Downing Street. Thanks to the wonders of modern technology he can still work and continue to tell us we're all fecked for the foreseeable. Pretty funny really!

An interesting thought however is that on the other side of this shit people might be a little more grateful for what we have. Before the virus everyone had it all so perfect that we had to make shit up to be upset about.

Virtue-signaling, social justice warriors, public shaming on Twitter and dickheads getting offended on behalf of other people they don't even know, just to prove their own morality.

How many wish we could just go back to arguing about Brexit? Just a thought, as I said.

Any idea when the pubs are open?

Coronavirus Files #2
Stupid or Grateful?

Funny how the world works out sometimes. On the radio there's a debate on whether the old Corona virus is the "great leveler" or not...

Would the bin men be in the same shitty old boat as the bankers?

Are the vegan sausage roll selling, socialist hippies gonna be sat in the same virtual dole queue next to the red wine, fillet steak eating, capitalist whores? All milking the government's giant milky tit in the sky for a few giro cheques as one...

I've no idea. I'm asking you for the answer if I'm being honest!

Whilst old 'Bo Jo' is recovering from the C-bomb in his countryside retreat, watching re-runs of

Ramsey's Kitchen Nightmares, eating foie gras, caviar and truffles washed down with Kopi Luwak coffee, wondering how the bollocks he's gonna get the country back-on-track...

... There's another poor sod living in a shared house in Crouch End, living week-to-week on a sixty-quid benefits cheque. Definitely won't be able to pay the rent as he's lost his job at Costa, thereby giving himself three months grace before being evicted by his prick of a landlord...

Who, incidentally, is shiting bricks as he owns four houses that he's worked his whole life to buy. The mortgage repayments are crippling and, with half his tenants unable to pay the rent, they may end up getting repossessed, thus leaving him penniless after forty years hard graft. He only wanted to leave his children some inheritance!

Then it goes on the wanker bankers - trillions in debt, but still giving bonuses to the fat cat cunts who go cap in hand to government asking for a bail out as they've bolloxed it all up....

Tough old times it's fair to say. Kinda glad I'm living in a caravan whilst the old dear's safely stranded in the land down under. Keep calm and carry on, I suppose.

I've heard it said (far more eloquently than I'm intentionally going to put it) that when the shit hits the fan, you can't control the fact there's shit everywhere. However, you can control your own response to the fact everything's covered in shit.

Thought process being that you're not in control of the circumstances, no matter how bad they may be. However, you are absolutely in charge of your attitude and how to go about improving yourself and your circumstances. Not the cards your dealt, more how you play them type vibe.

And gratitude plays a huge part in all that, old bean.

Grateful in the fact that even when things really do go tits up, you realise that when the worst does happen, there's a strange beauty and freedom to it.

Or something like that. Was kinda just thinking that an incident/infection at a Wuhan Seafood Market in lovely, lovely China had made me either a lot more stupid, or more grateful?

Probably both to be fair. Have a nice day!

CORONAVIRUS FILES #3
CONFUSED

Two months it'll be this Friday - living in a caravan in the woods that is. Settled into this countryside life rather well if I dare say so myself.

Two months into a pandemic that's never been seen before in mine - or anyone's - lifetime. Pure bubonic plague with a 'Keep Calm and Carry On' vibe, although we can't carry on as there's no bloody work..

Waiting on guidance from those Posho, Etonian Shitheads in charge to let us know what the score is with the old Coronavirus. How long those of us on the 'Rock N Roll' can keep claiming and those lucky sods getting furloughed can still get their 80% to chill at home.

Basically, it would be nice to know when we can go back to spending our hard-earned money on expensive craft lagers, talking utter shite and arguing about football.

Who remembers pubs? They were bloody great, weren't they!?

Nostalgia can be a broken record, but never when it comes to boozers...

Has to be said that old 'BoJo' definitely dropped a bollock the other day. A fifteen-minute speech in a fancy suit and hair as combed as it's ever gonna be essentially saying as follows:

"Go to work... actually don't go to work.... unless you can work from home. In that case don't go to work. Or possibly get the transport, if you have to travel, then go to work, but wear a helmet... and some garlic. Actually just use 'Great British common sense' - but remember only go outside two-metres away from yourself. OK? Great. Crack on!"

Well, thanks Boris - but that makes as much sense as waxing a goat, calling it Colin and ordering a kebab with extra chilli sauce from it. Maybe try considering what the feck you're actually trying to say next time. Even the Welsh made more sense than you!

It is however interesting to think that we're living through a moment in time that is going to be a significant part of our history.

Well worth considering this. In thirty years time – when your little goblin grandchildren are running around your webbed feet – are you going to be able say you acted with kindness and dignity during the Coronavirus pandemic, or were you one of those dickheads that stockpiled toilet paper in a caravan?

I'm probably leaning towards the latter.

As you were...

Coronavirus Files #4
Social Media is
Bollocks

Just over ten weeks now of caravan life in the woods and it would appear that the world has officially gone to shit. Along with the coronavirus running rampant globally, there are crazy race riots in America over the killing of George Floyd, down to yet another horrific incident of police brutality.

It would appear that the death of this poor man is the straw that broke the camels back. Looting, protests, riots, police officers getting shot and Donald Trump acting the bollocks, as per, with a bible in his hand.

Was only a few weeks ago that he suggested injecting industrial strength bleach as a cure. Turns out quite a few people tried that and the hospitals were inundated not only with Covid-19 patients, but they also had to deal with silly twats that had swallowed bleach.

The problem with social media is that it gives a voice to everyone and anyone, and while we still have labels on bleach saying 'DO NOT DRINK THIS', I'm not a hundred percent convinced that everyone should have a voice - as lets be honest: most people are fucking idiots.

I place myself firmly in that category by the way. I've never drunk bleach, however I have drunkenly pissed myself (whist trying to have a wee behind a bush), and I nearly choked to death on a sausage that I'd nicked.

So, as I'm sure you'll agree, I'm not the type of person you should be listening to on important economic or political factors, or really anything for that matter. In fact, put this book down and go do something productive with your life, dickhead...

Still here? Fair enough. I'll keep rambling.

Most iPhones are built in Shenzen, China, in a factory where conditions are so bad that the company Foxconn (who Apple hired to assemble the iPhones) make workers sign pledges stating they would not attempt to kill themselves. This is because in 2010 worker after worker threw themselves off the factory roof.

Its incredibly tragic, and essentially for what? So we can sit at home with a bucket of KFC and argue on Twitter, Facebook and Youtube!? Within ten seconds of looking at the comments on any of those, you're bound to witness people bitching at each other.

Arguing on your iPhone is similar to calling someone an abusive name when driving during a spat of road rage. There's generally no immediate consequence. You're in a big metal box with wheels that can speed off immediately after you've just called someone a 'Bollocking Knobhead'.

As a species, we're still in the embryonic stages of social media and haven't figured out how to use the bloody thing efficiently just yet. Here's to hoping we can figure out how to be just a little bit more kind to each other.

Still got no idea when the bloody pubs are opening up.

SHE ONLY FELT THIS WAY WHEN THE FULL MOON WAS OUT

She only felt this way when the full moon was out, mildly put out with a psychotic edge to proceedings. January wasn't helping either: the dark evenings, short days and ridiculous notion of 'Dry Jan'.

Without booze there's too many hours in the day, her dear old dad used to say. He also said he tangoed with a widow as she was running from the graveyard in '76. Who fuckin' knows?

Clearing her throat she attempts to sit down and read The Archetypes & The Collective Unconscious by that nutter Carl Jung. The early part of this New

Year was supposed to be here to clear out that space between the ears.

Get rid of all the darkness and twat some light in there. Eat kale, read philosophy (finally understand why old Sigmund was a misogynistic prick), lose half a stone and stop being the kind to buy shit they don't need to impress those they don't even like. You know the type.

Six days down and the boredom of a Saturday night in really drives it home. She ponders, *"who's ever really comfortable in on their own, if they're truly honest?"*

Previously the only time she craved solitude was when the hangover reached its crescendo. Fearing the White Wine Witch may have reared her ugly head the night before: phone off, door closed, light off and Netflix on. Aimlessly searching for some sappy American Rom-Com to fill the void and batter/shake off the hangover. The old routine, the whoring angel rising...

Can't concentrate. A brew always helps. Downstairs she flicks on the kettle, pulls out the Yorkshire Gold and ponders how many days left before she can join the girls getting shit faced. It's not the booze that's missing... it's how to kill the hours.

The Darkside of the Moon record clock on the wall says 9:00pm. Too early for bed.

The straying brain finds its way to the usual territory of the record collection, whilst stoically avoiding eye contact with that bottle of Merlot left by Mother Red Cap.

Calm the tide - it's only a month. Think of the poor sods in solitary confinement for thirty days. No nothing, let alone the demon drink. Just a hundred acres of hell to be seen before check out time.

Top five albums, that'll kill some time. Whack the needle down and watch them spin.

Springsteen has to makes an appearance with Nebraska. Blood on the Tracks by Dylan's up there. Pure Comedy by Father John jumps out and slaps a bitch. What next? Tapestry by Carole King always a worthy addition.

One more. Davie Boy Jones. Brixton's favourite son has got to be in there! Ziggy Stardust or Hunky Dory? Tough one...

The needle falls, the record spins and belts out that voice we've all heard in pubs, clubs, cars, shopping centres and dentists over the years.

The banging on the door starts again. Fourth time this week. Unconcerned as she knows its only that old lady complaining. Also well aware that HE'S two miles down the road, she can see his bloody fingers, wave and smile...

Chain on the door, close the curtains, ignoring the outside world, head inside your own. Through knockouts and blackouts, it's the best way.

Zoning into side two, the boredom's gone into the ether, along with the anxiety, stress and bollocks. It's a God Awful Small Affair, To The Girl With The Mousy Hair belts out across the room while she sings along to her favourite Bowie Song.

SCHOOL

"**O**'Reilly! Why haven't you done your bloody homework!? Five hundred words on Shakespeare's Hamlet were supposed to be on my desk first thing this morning boy!"

"I haven't done it, Mr. Mackey - and do not intend to"

"Right, that's it Boy! You've got a detention at lunchtime and a letter will be sent home to your Mother if I don't receive the essay first thing tomorrow morning!"

"Well, first thing's first, Mr. Mackey. I will not be attending any detentions, so you can get fucked - and you certainly will not be receiving five hundred words on Hamlet in the morning..."

"DO NOT ANSWER ME BACK, BOY! YOU WILL DO AS YOU ARE TOLD! HOW DARE YOU SWEAR AT ME!?!?"

"If you could possibly stop shouting, as it indicates a lack of vocabulary, Mr. Mackey - and allow me to explain. You see, after conducting my own research into the educational system, I believe it to be outdated. And, in protest to the outdated, draconian, protocols you seem so determined to live by, I will not be conforming any longer."

"YOU WILL DO AS YOU ARE TOLD BOY!"

"You're shouting again and it's somewhat uncouth. I can see you're struggling, so please allow me to explain further...

You see, the current public educational system was primarily based on the Prussian educational system - which incidentally is the same system the Japanese used before World War II...

Now, the purpose of the Prussian educational system was to produce good soldiers - and a good soldier is above all obedient, not autonomous. I'm sure you'll agree that a certain level of autonomy is vital in today's society in order for us to live competitive, focused lives and contribute to our ever-changing society..?"

Mr. Mackey is currently looking at O'Reilly like he's got two bent heads.

"Now, when this system of education spread into Europe in the 1800s, they weren't looking for good soldiers. In fact, they wanted workers as the Industrial Revolution was in full swing and schools were looking to raise good factory employees to help build the country...

Interestingly enough, that's why we have bells in schools. As the system was training school children sit in rows and work to the bell, all factory work-type ethos. Hence why it was logical to put school children through the same education process that you would put soldiers through...

The Industrial Revolution ended in 1880 and now it's 2020, so by my calculations I deem this current system to be outdated by one hundred and forty years. In summary, the educational system we use is tooled to produce obedient workers - not autonomous individuals - and is primarily a dogmatic ideology...

For this reason, I'm not writing shit all on that twat Shakespeare and his bollocks little 'Hamlet' play Mr. Mackey - so you can ram your homework up your hole!"

Mr. Mackey was hungover, hated his job on the best of days and didn't really understand any of what the little shit just said. He just felt this school was one big cunt farm.

The End

Printed in Great Britain
by Amazon

⌐058